Bubble and Squeak

by Jenny Dale

Illustrated by Susan Hellard

SCHOLASTIC INC.

New York   Toronto   London   Auckland   Sydney
Mexico City   New Delhi   Hong Kong   Buenos Aires

ISBN 0-439-79122-7

Text copyright © 2001 by Working Partners Limited
Illustrations copyright © 2001 by Susan Hellard

All rights reserved. Published by Scholastic Inc. 557 Broadway, New York, NY 10012, by arrangement with Macmillan Children's Books, London, England. JENNY DALE'S PUPPY TALES is a trademark of Working Partners Limited. SCHOLASTIC and associated logos are trademarks and/or registered trademarks of Scholastic Inc.

12 11 10 9 8 7 6 5 4 3 2 1   5 6 7 8 9 10/0

Printed in the U.S.A.
First printing, September 2005

Chapter One

"Come on in, Squeak!" Bubble barked, as he splashed around in the foamy bubbles. "The water's fine!"

"I don't want a bath," Squeak whined, his ears flat against his head. He backed into a corner and tried to make himself as small as possible.

"Look at the two of you — you're both filthy." Mary Connor, the pups' owner, was pouring dog shampoo over Bubble's muddy back. "You look more like two brown dogs than two white ones!"

"We were only playing, Mary," Bubble woofed, snapping at a bubble that floated up into the air. "We rolled in the mud, and we had a *great* time!"

"But now we have to take another horrible *bath*," Squeak whimpered. Miserably, he plumped down on his fat little bottom and put his head on his paws. It was all right for

Bubble — he loved baths. Squeak hated them even more than he hated going to the vet!

"I hope I can get you both clean before Dad sees you," Mary said, looking worried. She lifted Bubble out and began to dry him with an old towel.

"Yes, Squeak, we don't want Mr. Connor to see that we got dirty *again*," Bubble yapped anxiously. "You know he doesn't like it."

Squeak's heart sank. He knew Bubble was right. He'd have to take a bath, or Mr. Connor would be angry. Mary's dad didn't think Bubble and Squeak were the right kind of dogs to live on a busy farm. Until a few weeks ago, the puppy twins had lived in a house with their mom, Molly, and her owner, Mr. Nolan. Then Mary had arrived with her mom and dad to pick them up. . . .

"Oh, they're gorgeous!" Mary said.
Bubble and Squeak rushed over to meet her, their tails wagging. Mary's voice was soft, and she handled the pups gently when she stroked them.

"She's nice!" Squeak woofed.

"I like her!" Bubble barked.

Mrs. Connor looked nice, too.

But Mr. Connor stood there frowning. "They're *white*," he said. "I thought they'd be brown, like Molly."

Mr. Nolan shrugged. "Well, they're the only ones left from the litter."

Bubble and Squeak looked at each other, then crept away to hide behind their mom. They weren't sure why Mr. Connor didn't like their white coats.

"With all the rain and mud, they'll be filthy all the time," Mr. Connor went on.

"Oh, Dad," Mary said. She picked the pups up, hugging one

in each arm. "I'll keep them clean. I'll give them a bath whenever they need it!"

"Bath?" Squeak gave a puzzled woof. "What's that?"

"They *are* very cute, John," Mary's mom added.

Mr. Connor sighed and nodded his head.

"Thanks, Dad!" Mary cried. She rushed over to kiss him, still carrying the two pups. . . .

The trouble was, Mr. Connor was right, Squeak thought. It *was* difficult for him and his brother to stay clean on the farm. There were just too many tempting puddles and muddy fields and damp ditches!

And when they got muddy, Mary had to bathe them in the big sink in the shed before they were allowed in the kitchen.

"Come on, Squeak," Mary said, as she finished drying Bubble. "It's your turn now."

"No-o-o-o!" Squeak howled as Mary bent to pick him up.

Just then, the shed door opened. Squeak's eyes lit up. This was his chance! He wriggled away from Mary and made a dash for it.

Mary and Bubble jumped up to chase after him, and Mary accidentally knocked the soap dish and sent it flying.

"Oh, no, you don't, Squeak!" A firm hand grasped the scruff of Squeak's neck, just as he reached the doorway. "Here's the little rascal, Mary." Mr. Connor handed a whimpering Squeak to his daughter. "And make sure he doesn't get away this time — aaargh!"

Mary's dad slipped on the bar of soap that had fallen to the floor. He skidded forward and went headfirst into the sink full of bubbles.

Chapter Two

Mr. Connor wiped the suds from his face. "I *knew* these two pups would be trouble!" he shouted angrily.

"Sorry, Dad!" Mary cried. "I knocked over the soap dish when Squeak escaped."

"Well, either they keep clean

from now on, or they'll have to live outside — and I mean it this time!" Mr. Connor stomped off across the farmyard.

Squeak looked at Bubble in dismay. Mr. Connor sounded really serious. And now Mary was in trouble, too. "OK, I'll take a bath now," he whimpered. "But we'd better not get dirty tomorrow."

"What do you want to do today?" Squeak yapped.

It was the following morning. Mary was eating breakfast before going to school. The puppies were waiting hopefully for tidbits under the kitchen table.

"We could chase the ducks

around the farmyard," Bubble woofed, wagging his tail cheerfully. "And then we could go into the field and find some nice mud to roll in. And then we could find a big puddle and —"

"No, no, *no*!" Squeak barked. "You heard what Mr. Connor said. He'll make us live outside if we get dirty again so soon."

"But we're dogs — and dogs *like* getting dirty," Bubble pointed out.

"I know." Squeak nipped his brother's ear playfully. "But Mr. Connor doesn't like it."

"So?" Bubble jumped on Squeak. "Mr. Connor isn't very clean himself after he's worked on the farm all day, is he? He stinks!"

"But at least Mr. Connor likes taking baths," Squeak panted, as he and Bubble rolled over and over underneath the table. "*I* don't! So let's try to keep clean from now on," he growled, pinning Bubble to the ground.

"What are those two up to?" Mr. Connor peered under the table.

"They're just playing, Dad." Mary laughed as the two pups sat up and shook themselves.

"Would you hurry up, Mary, and finish your breakfast, please?" Mrs. Connor said. "You, too, John."

"But, Barbie, I just now sat down to my bacon and eggs!" Mary's dad said grumpily.

"Well, I have to start the cleaning,

John," said Mrs. Connor. "This house is a terrible mess."

Mary and her father looked at each other. "Mrs. Riley!" they groaned.

Mary's mom looked flustered. "Well, yes, Mrs. Riley *is* coming to visit this afternoon."

"Great! Mrs. Riley!" Bubble woofed. "She brought a yummy cake last time and dropped lots of crumbs!"

"I remember!" Squeak woofed back. "I wonder what she'll bring this time?"

"Not that woman again," Mary's dad grumbled. "All she does is brag about how much money she has."

"And she's really snooty, too,"

Mary added, slipping two small pieces of toast under the table.

"Hey, you grabbed the bigger piece!" Bubble yapped as Squeak wolfed it down.

"Well, she *is* a neighbor," Mrs. Connor muttered. She began to wipe the kitchen table.

"Can I finish my breakfast before you clean my plate?" Mary's dad said, as Mrs. Connor picked up his plate of bacon and eggs and wiped the table underneath it.

"Mom, will you keep Bubble and Squeak inside today, please?" Mary asked. She picked up her backpack. "I don't want them getting dirty again."

"Yes, but they'd better not get

under my feet," Mrs. Connor said. "I'm going to be very busy."

"I don't want to stay inside," Squeak whined as he and Bubble went to see Mary safely out of the house, as they did every morning.

"Bye, Bubble. Bye, Squeak." Mary kissed each pup in turn. "Be good!"

"At least we'll keep clean if we stay inside, Squeak," Bubble pointed out.

Squeak wagged his tail more cheerfully. "That's true."

"And there are loads of games we can play inside," Bubble woofed. "Come on, let's go and play Hide Mr. Connor's Slippers!"

The pups raced each other up the stairs.

But Mrs. Connor had gotten there before them and was dusting the bedroom furniture. "Out!" she said irritably.

Bubble and Squeak whined as Mrs. Connor shut the door, leaving them on the landing.

"I know," Squeak barked. "Let's go play Hide Under Mary's Rug!"

That was one of their favorite games. One of the pups would crawl under the rug on Mary's bedroom floor, while the other one pounced on him every time he moved. It was so much fun.

But not for long. The pups had hardly started their game before Mrs. Connor bustled in with her duster.

"Out you go!" she said briskly.

"It's not fair!" Squeak whined, but Mrs. Connor put them outside and then closed the door *again*.

It was the same all morning. Whenever the pups tried to play a quiet game of Chew the Bath Mat or Running Up and Down the Stairs Very Fast, Mrs. Connor put a stop to it.

"We can't do *anything*," Squeak whined as they sat in the hall. They'd been shut out of every single room in the farmhouse.

"Well, maybe we could *help* Mrs. Connor instead of playing games," Bubble woofed. "Look!"

Mrs. Connor was battling with some kind of monster that had been hiding in the closet under the stairs. Bubble and Squeak both growled and bared their teeth. She would *definitely* need their help now. It was their duty to protect Mary and her family from this big noisy monster!

"Grrr! We're ready for you!" Bubble barked. He dashed down the hall toward Mrs. Connor. "I'll bark at you until you stop making that horrible noise!"

"And I'll bite you!" Squeak growled. He grabbed one end of the monster and hung on to it as Mrs. Connor tried to push it along.

"All right, that's it! I can't even vacuum in peace," Mrs. Connor said angrily. She stormed over to the back door and opened it. "Outside — NOW!"

The pups trailed gloomily out into the farmyard.

"Doesn't Mrs. Connor know we're trying to help?" Bubble yapped as he sniffed the air. It had been raining, and everything smelled cool and damp.

"Remember what we said about keeping clean, Bubble!" Squeak woofed anxiously. The farmyard was awash with mud, and there were lots of puddles.

"Oh, yes. . . ." Bubble's eyes lit up. He'd noticed a really *big* puddle, right next to them.

"We don't want to live outside in a kennel, do we?" Squeak reminded him.

"No," Bubble agreed. But the puddle looked so deep, he just *had* to jump right into the middle of it — and he splashed Squeak from head to toe.

"You did that on purpose!" Squeak whined as Bubble ran off, barking gleefully.

Squeak chased his brother

through every puddle in the farmyard. Soon, both pups were soaked and filthy. They headed off into one of the fields, where Bubble found some even thicker mud to roll around in. It had been churned up by Mr. Connor's tractor.

"I'm hungry!" Squeak whined when they were covered in mud from head to toe.

"So am I," woofed Bubble. He headed back to the farmhouse. Squeak followed.

As usual, the back door was propped open. The two pups charged into the kitchen, leaving muddy pawprints on the clean floor.

Bubble stopped and sniffed

the air. "I can smell someone different," he yapped. "Mrs. Riley must be here!"

Squeak didn't reply. He was too busy stealing a dog biscuit from Bubble's bowl.

"Hey, I was saving that for later," Bubble barked grumpily. Squeak took to his heels, still carrying the biscuit in his mouth, and headed for the living room.

A woman in fancy clothes sat on the sofa next to Mrs. Connor. It was Mrs. Riley. She looked around the room and sniffed snootily. "It must be *very* difficult, trying to keep things clean on a farm," she said. "I do feel sorry for you, Barbie."

Mrs. Connor turned a little red. "Oh, it's not too bad," she said.

Mrs. Riley looked at Mary's mom. "You should see *my* house," she said. "It's spotless. But, then, of course I *do* have a cleaning lady and a housekeeper."

"More tea?" Mrs. Connor asked grumpily, picking up the tea tray. "I'll just run into the kitchen and put the kettle on again."

Right at that moment, Squeak barged into the living room, followed by Bubble. Mrs. Connor was just behind the door, and the tray was knocked right out of her hands.

"Oh!" Mrs. Connor gasped as everything crashed to the floor.

Bubble and Squeak didn't even notice. They were too busy greeting the visitor.

"Have you brought anything nice to eat?" Bubble barked. "That cake you brought last time was yummy!" He jumped up at Mrs. Riley and left muddy pawprints all over her skirt.

"I bet there's something nice in here!" Squeak yapped. He stuck his nose into Mrs. Riley's big shiny handbag. He was so excited, he dropped the dog biscuit inside it.

"Help!" Mrs. Riley screamed. "Get these filthy little dogs away from me!"

Chapter Three

"It was your fault for jumping in that puddle, Squeak!" Bubble whined.

"No, it was *yours* for finding all that nice mud to roll in!" Squeak whimpered.

The puppies were in disgrace.

Mrs. Riley had stormed out of

the farmhouse, and Mary's mom had had to clean up all the mess. But first she'd shut the pups in an empty pigpen.

"And you can stay there till Mary comes home from school!" Mrs. Connor had said angrily, slamming the door shut.

Bubble and Squeak huddled together in a corner of the smelly pen, feeling very worried. What would Mary say when she saw them? What would Mr. Connor say?

"Don't worry, Squeak." Bubble licked his brother's nose. "Mary will give us a bath, and everything will be OK."

"*Another* bath," Squeak whined. He shivered.

Suddenly, Bubble sat up and sniffed the air. "It's Mary!" he barked.

A moment later, Mary popped her head over the side of the pen. "Look at you two!" she said. "You're both filthy, and Mom's really angry."

Bubble and Squeak huddled together sadly, their stumpy tails between their legs.

Mary sighed, shaking her head. Then she let herself into the pen and picked them both up for a cuddle.

Bubble licked her ear. "We're very sorry, Mary," he woofed softly.

"At least *you* don't mind if we're dirty or not," Squeak

whimpered as he snuffled his nose into Mary's neck.

Mr. and Mrs. Connor came out into the farmyard. They both looked furious. Bubble's and Squeak's hearts sank.

"Put those pups down, Mary!" Mrs. Connor said sharply. "You'll get your school clothes dirty."

Mary quickly put Bubble and Squeak down on the ground. "I'm really sorry about what happened, Mom," she said.

"I've never been so embarrassed in my life," Mrs. Connor went on. "And in front of Mrs. Riley, too."

"This is their last chance, Mary," Mr. Connor said sternly. "If the pups can't keep themselves clean, they really will have to live outside in a kennel. And they won't be allowed in the house at all. I've had enough."

Bubble and Squeak looked at each other and whimpered. They didn't want to live in a horrible old kennel. They wanted to be with Mary in the farmhouse. They wanted to sleep on Mary's bed. And sit under the kitchen table waiting for tidbits. And curl up in front of the fire in the living room — like they always did.

As Mary went off to fill the shed sink with water, Squeak yapped at his brother. "Bubble, we've just *got* to keep clean from now on."

"I know," Bubble yapped in agreement. "Don't worry, it'll be easy!"

* * *

But it *wasn't* easy. It rained a lot —
and that made the farmyard even
muddier. Mary helped all she
could. When she took Bubble and
Squeak out for their morning
walk, she carried them over the
muddiest puddles. But she
couldn't help when she was at
school.

"Look out for that puddle,
Squeak!" Bubble barked, as they
took a stroll around the farmyard
the following afternoon.

Squeak tiptoed carefully around
it. He couldn't help staring at
the puddle as he did so. He
was longing to jump in and
splash around. But he knew

31

Mary would be upset, so he didn't.

"Yaaah! Can't catch me!" One of the ducks scurried past on its way to the pond, quacking loudly.

Bubble was about to chase after it when Squeak grabbed his tail.

"No, Bubble!" he barked. "Look at the mud around the pond!"

Bubble growled a little, then gave up on the duck-chasing idea.

The two pups raced back into the farmhouse, where it was a lot safer.

At least, they *thought* they were safe.

While Bubble was sniffing around the big open fireplace, a shower of soot fell down the chimney. It came very near to covering him in black dust. Luckily, Bubble jumped out of the way, just in time.

"We can't go *anywhere* or do *anything*!" Squeak yapped. "There's dirt all over the place!"

"But just think how happy Mary will be that we're still white!" Bubble barked.

And he was right. Mary was really pleased when she came home from school and saw her two clean puppies. "Great job, boys!" she cried, giving them both a hug.

But Bubble and Squeak couldn't help feeling worried. This was only the first day, and it had been *really* difficult. How on earth were they going to keep it up?

Chapter Four

"Bubble and Squeak have been
very good, haven't they, Mom?"
Mary asked proudly.

   She was sitting with her mom in
the living room, watching TV.
The pups were curled up together
in one big fluffy white ball on her

lap. "They've stayed clean for a whole week."

"And it was really difficult, too," Bubble yapped.

"But at least it means no baths!" Squeak woofed.

The pups had spent most of their time playing and sleeping in Mary's bedroom, where they felt safe. It was very boring staying inside all the time, but at least they hadn't gotten dirty.

Mrs. Connor put her knitting down as the program finished and the commercials began. "Well, let's hope it lasts," she said. "I'll go and put the kettle on. Your dad should be home from the market soon."

"I bet you're the first one to get

dirty!" Squeak yapped. He gave his brother a little nip.

"No, I bet *you* are!" Bubble nipped him back, and they started rolling around together on Mary's lap.

"New Kleener-than-Kleen's wonderful *bubbles* will make your hair *squeaky* clean!" said a loud voice.

Bubble and Squeak stopped rolling around and sat still, their ears perked up.

"Someone said our names!" Bubble barked.

"Who was it?" Squeak yapped.

Mary was laughing. "Look, Mom!" she said, as Mrs. Connor paused in the doorway. "The pups heard their names on the TV!"

Bubble and Squeak knew what the TV was. It was that strange box in the corner of the room that had lots of people and sometimes even other dogs inside it. They stared at the screen.

A woman was shaking her long hair around and holding a big green bottle. "It's true!" she said. "Kleener-than-Kleen's

bubbles really *do* make your hair squeaky clean!"

Bubble and Squeak began to bark when they heard their names again. "She's talking about us!"

Mary grinned. "Maybe we should get some Kleener-than-Kleen shampoo for Bubble and Squeak!" she joked. "Not that they need it," she added quickly, as her mom frowned. "They're being so good right now. They're already cleaner than clean!"

Bubble and Squeak looked at each other proudly. They were cleaner than clean! That wasn't bad for two pups who had been in trouble for being filthy just a week ago. Now all they had to do was keep it up. . . .

A few days later, Mrs. Connor was hanging some laundry out to dry.

"I hope you pups are going to be careful," she said with a frown.

The sun had come out — but it had been raining for hours and hours, and the farmyard was full of muddy puddles.

"Of *course* we're going to be careful!" Bubble sniffed, as Mrs. Connor picked up the laundry basket and went inside.

"What should we do now?" Squeak woofed.

"Let's wait by the gate for Mary to come home from school," Bubble yapped back.

"OK," Squeak agreed.

But as they were making their way over to the gate, something happened. A huge gust of wind blew across the farmyard. It tugged a yellow T-shirt off the clothesline and carried it away.

Bubble didn't notice, but Squeak did. "Oh, no!" he barked. "That's Mary's favorite T-shirt!"

Determined to get the T-shirt back, Squeak chased after it. *Splash!* He ran through one muddy puddle. *Splash!* And another.

"Squeak! Be careful!" Bubble yelped, horrified.

Suddenly, the wind died down for a moment, and the T-shirt fell to the ground.

Squeak rushed toward it through the mud. He grabbed it in his teeth. "Goth ith!" he woofed. It was hard to woof with a T-shirt in his mouth.

"And the mud's got *you*!" Bubble whined, rushing over to him. "Squeak, you're *filthy*!"

Chapter Five

Squeak looked down at himself. He *was* dirty. In fact, he was dirtier than dirty! He dropped the T-shirt back on the ground. "Bubble, what are we going to do?" he whimpered. "If Mr. and Mrs. Connor see me like this, we'll never be allowed in the house again."

"And Mary will be really upset," Bubble added. Then his ears perked up, and his tail started to wag. "I have a brilliant idea!"

Squeak's ears perked up, too. "What?" he asked.

"*I'll* bathe you!" Bubble barked.

"Oh, no!" Squeak lay his ears flat against his head and backed away from his brother. "No way!" he woofed.

"Do you have any better ideas?" Bubble yapped sternly.

Squeak looked glum. "No," he sniffed.

"Come on, then," Bubble woofed. He turned and headed toward the stables on the other side of the farmyard.

Squeak picked up Mary's T-shirt and followed his brother.

"I can't bathe you in the shed sink," Bubble woofed as he ran, "because I can't turn on the faucet. But I know where there is some water already poured."

He stopped by one of the troughs that were full of drinking

water for the horses. "You'll have to take a bath in there!"

Squeak dropped the T-shirt again, then howled. "But that's for the *horses*. And, anyway, you can't bathe me — you don't have any soap!"

Bubble cocked his head to one side. "You're right, Squeak," he woofed. "I'll go get some." He dashed off toward the house.

Mrs. Connor was on the phone when Bubble sneaked in, so she didn't see him run up the stairs and into the bathroom.

Panting, Bubble stopped and looked around. He couldn't see the doggy soap Mary always used when she bathed them. But there was a big green bottle on the side of the bathtub. Bubble had seen that same bottle on the TV. It was Kleener-than-Kleen! Mrs. Connor must have bought it when she went shopping the day before.

Perfect, Bubble thought. He grabbed the bottle in his teeth and hurried outside again.

Squeak was waiting by the horse trough, shivering.

Bubble dropped the bottle on the ground. "Help me get the top off, Squeak," he yapped.

First Squeak stuffed Mary's T-shirt safely under the trough, where it couldn't blow away again. Then Bubble held the bottle between his paws while

Squeak twisted the top off with his teeth.

"In you go, Squeak," Bubble yapped firmly after he'd poured a drop of shampoo into the trough.

"Do I *have* to?" Squeak whimpered.

"Yes, you do!" Bubble barked. Then he took another look at his brother. Squeak really was FILTHY! He poured some more shampoo into the trough. This time, half the bottle went in. "Come on. Mary will be home from school soon," he added.

Slowly, Squeak climbed into the trough. "Ooh! It's fre-e-e-e-zing!" he howled as the cold water touched his tummy.

"Make sure you roll around

and get all the dirt off," Bubble yapped.

Shivering, Squeak began to roll around in the water. But, all of a sudden, something happened! Bubbles began to appear. Hundreds and hundreds — and HUNDREDS of them. And they kept on coming.

The bubbles began to cover Squeak completely. "Help!" he spluttered. "Help! There's a Bubble Monster in here, and it's attacking me!"

"Oh, no!" Bubble yelped as Squeak disappeared under a mound of bubbles. "What am I going to do? I've *got* to save Squeak from the Bubble Monster."

Chapter Six

The bubbles in the trough were getting higher and higher and foamier and foamier all the time.

"Don't worry, Squeak!" Bubble barked. "I'll get help!" He shot away across the farmyard, splashing through all the puddles and the thick mud. He was about to run toward the house. But, suddenly, he spotted Mary and her mom walking up the lane. Mrs. Connor must have gone to meet Mary at the school bus, and they were almost home.

"Mary!" Bubble barked at the top of his voice, sticking his head through the gate. "Mary, come quick! The Bubble Monster's attacking Squeak, and I don't know what to do!"

"Bubble!" Mary ran toward him. "What's the matter? Where's Squeak?"

"Quick!" Bubble danced around Mary's ankles as she came through the gate. "Follow me!" And he dashed back to the stables.

Mary and Mrs. Connor followed.

They stopped and stared when they saw the horse trough absolutely overflowing with bubbles. There was so much foam that Squeak was nowhere to be seen.

"What's happened?" Mary asked, looking confused. But, just then, a little head appeared from the middle of the bubbles.

"Mary!" Squeak whimpered. "Save me!"

"It's Squeak!" Mary cried, and hurried to the rescue. She plunged her arms into the trough and pulled the little dog out. Squeak was covered in foam and couldn't stop sneezing.

"Squeak, are you all right?" Bubble barked.

Just then, Mr. Connor brought one of the horses into the stables. "What on earth's going on here?" he said.

Bubble whined. In his dash to get help for Squeak, he had gotten pretty muddy himself.

Squeak snuggled even closer to Mary and buried his wet, foamy face in her shoulder. They'd had their very last chance, and from now on Mr. Connor would make them live outside in a cold kennel.

"Look!" Mary noticed the bottle of shampoo lying on the ground. "Bubble, were you trying to bathe Squeak because he got dirty?"

"You're not telling me those

pups have been trying to bathe *themselves*?" Mr. Connor said. Then he burst out laughing.

"I think they have!" said Mrs. Connor. She was smiling, too.

"It's not funny!" Squeak barked angrily, still clinging to Mary. "I was nearly eaten by the Bubble Monster!"

Mary picked up the bottle. "No wonder there were so many bubbles." She grinned. "This is Extra Foamy Kleener-than-Kleen!"

Her mom and dad laughed even harder.

"I wonder how Squeak managed to get so dirty in the first place," Mary said. Then she spotted something yellow tucked underneath the trough. She put Squeak down and picked it up. "It's my T-shirt!"

"I hung that out on the line this afternoon," Mrs. Connor said. "What's it doing there?"

Mary gasped. "Maybe it blew away and Squeak rescued it!" she said. "That could be why he's dirty! And maybe Bubble got muddy when he ran for help."

"These two are quite a pair!" said Mr. Connor. He was still roaring with laughter. "You never know what they're going to be up to next!"

Bubble's and Squeak's hopes rose. Mr. Connor wasn't angry. And Mrs. Connor wasn't, either.

Maybe the pups hadn't lost their last chance after all.

"Dad, Mom, you're not going to make Bubble and Squeak live outside now, are you?" Mary asked.

Two pairs of big brown eyes stared at Mr. and Mrs. Connor. Bubble and Squeak waited to hear what they would say.

"Well. . . ." Mr. Connor looked down at the pups. "I've kind of got used to having them around the house. I think I'd miss them if they lived outside." He looked at Mary's mom.

Mrs. Connor thought for a while. "If the pups did come into the house, Mrs. Riley would never visit us again," she said. Then she grinned. "But really, I don't care at all! I've had enough of that Mrs. Riley's snooty ways!" She turned to Mary. "So, as long as Bubble and Squeak stay clean for *most* of the time, they can live inside," she agreed.

"Yes!" Bubble woofed happily. "Squeak, we don't have to live outside in a horrible old kennel!"

"Hurray!" Squeak barked, and wriggled to be let down.

Mary put Squeak back on the ground, and the two pups raced around in circles, chasing each other's tails. Everything had worked out fine.

"Hey, Squeak!" Bubble playfully nipped his brother's ear and then ran off. "Kleener-than-Kleen really does make you SQUEAKY clean!"

"That's an awful joke, Bubble!" Squeak woofed, chasing his brother across the farmyard.

"Look out for the puddles, boys!" Mary called after them.

Bubble and Squeak had stopped right on the edge of a big puddle of very dirty water.

"Mrs. Connor *did* say she didn't mind if we got a *little* dirty," Bubble woofed, staring at it.

"Should we?" Squeak barked naughtily.

They both turned around. Mary and her mom and dad were watching.

"We'd better not," Bubble yapped.

"All right, then," Squeak barked back. "We'll save it till tomorrow!"